Ready, Regan?

ALISON LEVEY

ILLUSTRATED BY KARYN LEWIS

READY, REGAN?
Text © 2019 by Alison Levey
All Rights Reserved

ISBN-13: 9781090798633

Published by KDP

For more background on the origin of the tool kit, other works in progress, and Alison's insights as a college academic advisor, visit her website at www.alisonlevey.com. For information and permission to reproduce selections from this book, please contact the author at rhymeswithchevy@gmail.com. Thank you for your interest.

Illustrations and cover design by Karyn Lewis Illustration. www.karynlewis.com

Editing by Editing Genie
www.editing-genie.com

For Brian, because he always believed.

Stay curious and be just a little bit brave and you'll always be ready for ANYthing!!

♡, Alison Levey
8.22.2020.

CHAPTER ONE

Regan Hines bounced impatiently along an imaginary hopscotch court as she waited for the school bus to arrive at her corner. As she hopped, she mentally crossed off all the items on her school supply list. Had she packed everything she needed into her new purple backpack? Scissors? Hop. Pencils? Hop. Notebooks, folders? Hop, hop. Ruler, markers? Turn! She knew she had that ruler, because it poked her in the back every time she jumped.

Finally, the school bus cleared the top of the hill two blocks away, and Regan let out a small yelp. Soon the brakes hissed and the doors squeaked open in front of Regan. Her mom—who'd been chasing Regan's little brother, Sam, around their maple tree—scooped him up and moved in for a quick group hug.

Regan scrambled up the steps without a backward glance.

"Happy Tuesday, and welcome back Regan!" said the driver, Mr. Schultz. Too anxious to answer, Regan just smiled and sat down in the third seat on the right side to wait for the next stop. Mr. Schultz had barely opened the door before Regan's best friend, Leslie—a tall girl with a long braid and a wide smile—had him locked in a bear hug.

"I missed you, Mr. Schultz," Leslie said, before plopping down next to Regan. "Aren't you excited about school today?" she asked. "And, oh my gosh, wait until you see my fancy new lunchbox—it's ah-mazing!"

The boys in the seat behind them rolled their eyes.

Regan leaned close to Leslie and whispered, "I always get a little nervous on the first day of school."

"What's to be nervous about? It's just school," said Leslie too loudly. "We're in third grade now, so we've basically been going to school fuh-ever. Second grade was easy-peasy. How much tougher can third grade be?"

"Leslie, first days just aren't my favorite, okay? New teacher, new information, new tests to take…" Her voice trailed off as her nerves got the best of her.

"Yeah, but some stuff never changes. Same name tag on your desk, same announcements you can't understand, same lining up, blah, blah, blah." Leslie took a breath. "Plus, new teacher? You can't be worried about Ms. Eaton. She was Hope's favorite of all time."

Hope was Leslie's big sister. She sometimes babysat Regan and Sam.

"Hope says she's super nice, her projects are super fun, and she loved Writing Workshop. Besides, teachers always love you, Regan. You never turn your homework in late or forget your jacket on the way to recess. Last year, almost every time we lined up, Mrs. Hoffman would say, 'I see Regan's ready', before she mentioned anyone else."

Regan smiled to herself as the bus pulled

into the Westbriar School parking lot. She was modest enough not to say anything except, "Well, I do try to be ready."

The girls skipped off the bus and up the front steps, nearly running into their principal, Mrs. Martino.

"Regan and Leslie, what a surprise to see the two of you together," she said with a wink. "Welcome back."

"Nice to see you too, Mrs. Martino," Regan said politely.

"Yep, glad to be here," Leslie called over her shoulder as the girls entered the building. They pushed through the swarm of students and found their new classroom on the second floor. Ms. Eaton welcomed them warmly and asked them to find their seats. No sooner had they turned to read the nametags than a body bolted

behind them, knocking Regan flat across the table in front of her.

"Quit blocking the way, you two! Bet I find my seat before you, Regan."

In unison, Regan and Leslie said, "Good grief, Conor!" and exchanged looks of annoyance. Leslie shook her head and mouthed, "Sorry about him," as she claimed her seat at the first table. Conor was Leslie's twin brother. For the life of her, Regan could not figure out how her best friend and her biggest pest could be in the same family—much less twins—but they were. Conor always managed to turn everything into a competition with Regan. It didn't seem to faze Leslie, but it drove Regan crazy. And yes, he found his place first. But instead of being annoyed, Regan was relieved. At least he wasn't at her table. Putting her backpack down, she noticed a note on the board.

Welcome to our 3rd Grade Adventure. Please:

1) Place all your supplies for this exciting journey on top of your desk.

2) Put your lunch in the bucket by the door.

3) Hang your backpack on your assigned hook in the closet.

I can't wait to get started. How about you?

         — Ms. Eaton

Soon the whole class had arrived. They got

busy getting organized. Regan was in charge of the buckets for glue sticks and extra pencils. They labeled their colorful folders with each subject and stacked the tissue boxes back by the sink. They signed up on the job chart, and each table group chose a name. Regan's group picked Blue Dolphins, and a cool glittered sign now hung above their table. They ate lunch, played tag at recess, and met the new librarian. Mrs. Sherry previewed two books even Regan hadn't already read. With ten minutes left before the closing bell, Ms. Eaton asked, "Does everyone have their tool kit ready?"

Tool kit? No mention had been made all day about a tool kit. Regan felt her chest tighten.

That wasn't on the supply list, she thought. *I'm sure I didn't miss anything.* She mentally checked off the items again, as if she hadn't already done that a dozen times over the weekend. There must be some mistake. Was it possible she was *not* ready? Regan scanned the room. She was relieved to see her classmates all looked as confused as she felt—even Conor.

Ms. Eaton laughed. "Silly me, I haven't given them to you yet. Of course, you're not ready." She pulled out a box full of colorful paper bags tied shut with bright ribbons. She asked Trevor and Maria to help her pass out the bags to the class.

"Put these right into your backpacks. Don't open them until you get home. Inside, there are four tools you need to have an awesome year in third grade. Your homework is to figure out how you'll use them. We'll get started on them first thing tomorrow morning."

Regan couldn't wait to open her tool kit. She

tried to guess what was inside as she carefully placed it in her backpack. She felt some paper and something small but very solid. She was afraid to press too hard in case any of it was breakable. Just then the closing bell rang, and Ms. Eaton called out, "Riders for Buses 2, 3, and 4 are free to go."

In the hallway, Leslie and Regan clasped hands and race walked toward the front doors of the school. Regan kept yanking on Leslie's arm to slow her down. The hall patrols had sent them back to start over more than once last year since Leslie did everything at full speed.

Once the bus was underway, Leslie turned to Regan and said, "Ms. Eaton sure gives crazy homework. I don't remember Hope getting a tool kit. Let's open them."

Regan grabbed Leslie's hand as she started

pulling on the zipper of her backpack. "Don't. I'm dying to know what's in it too, but Ms. Eaton said to wait until we got home. What if you drop something and it rolls to the back of the bus? Mr. Schultz will get angry if you get up while the bus is moving."

"Regan, why are you such a worrywart? That isn't going to happen. C'mon let go of my hand."

"Well, what if Conor sees you and tells Ms. Eaton we broke the rules? You know Conor would rat us out in a second. He'd love to get me in trouble on the first day of school."

"Okay, okay, you win. I'll wait until I get home. How exciting can it be? It's a pretty small bag, and it is homework after all."

With that, the bus came to a screeching halt, and Regan heard the front doors creak open. Yikes, this was her stop already. She stood up in a hurry and almost knocked over a nervous kindergartner. "Oops, sorry," she mumbled as she struggled with her backpack.

"Bye, Leslie, see you tomorrow." Leslie yelled something in reply but Regan was already off the bus and didn't hear her. She just waved as the bus pulled away.

Despite her awkward exit from the bus, it was a relief to be home. The suspense really was killing her. She greeted her mom, saying, "C'mon, Mom, I've got to get inside and start my homework."

"Homework? On your first day?" Her mom sighed. "It's going to be a busy year."

Once inside the house, Regan pulled the brightly colored bag out of her backpack. She held it over her head to keep out of Sam's reach.

"Honey, what is that?" asked her mom, trying hard to be heard over Sam's chant of, "Lemme see, lemme see, pweez."

"Oh, Mom," she said. "It's my tool kit, of course. Ms. Eaton gave them to us at the end of the day. I have to figure out what all the tools are for by tomorrow."

"A tool kit? Well, that's different," said her mom. "But sweetie, I'm afraid that's going to have to wait. Aren't you forgetting something? Earth to Regan!"

Regan looked up distractedly. She'd somehow gotten the ribbon in a knot and was struggling to open her tool kit.

"Black and white ball? Running? Kicking? Scoring? Ringing any bells?"

"Oh my gosh, I totally forgot. It's the first day of soccer practice!" Regan slid off her chair. "I'd better go get changed right away."

Regan flew upstairs to her room. She went immediately to the third drawer of her dresser where she kept all her shorts. She pulled out her favorite pair of black soccer shorts with the red stripes down the side. Opening the second drawer, she dug around for a few seconds and then yelled, "Mom, have you seen my soccer socks with the red...?" She heard a small cough behind her. Sam was standing at her bedroom door holding one long black sock in each hand.

"Sam, where did you find those? Did Mom put them in your drawer by mistake?"

Sam just grinned, took a big step backwards, turned, and ran toward the stairs yelling, "Catch me. Catch me!"

"Sam," Regan howled as she took off in hot pursuit, "get back here with those. C'mon buddy,

I need to get to practice." Sam was small, but he was quick. He was down the stairs and out of Regan's sight before she hit the landing.

"Sam, seriously. This is NOT funny," she yelled as she hit the tile foyer floor and rounded the corner into the kitchen. She still couldn't see Sam, but she heard him giggling. She saw one foot, with her soccer sock dangling off it, sticking out from behind the island. She also saw her mom sneaking in from the opposite side.

Mom reached Sam first. In no time at all the two of them were on the floor in a tickle match that made it easy for Regan to grab her socks.

"Gimme those, Sam," she said a little more harshly than necessary. Sam looked crushed, and her mom raised one eyebrow.

"What? He's making me late."

"He's doing no such thing. We'll be fine. He's

just having some fun with the big sister he missed all day long. Now, grab your snack and water bottle. The rest of your gear is in the backseat, so we're all ready to go. C'mon, Sam. Climb up and I'll give you a piggy back ride to the car."

"Yippee, giddy up," said Sam smiling again.

Regan petted her brother like a horse and whispered, "Sorry for snapping, Sam-man."

Chapter Two

They arrived at the field almost exactly 20 minutes later, on time as Mrs. Hines had predicted. Regan had managed to get her shin guards and cleats on in the car. Her mom put the car in park and turned around to look at Regan. "I'm going to talk to Mrs. Lewis about the snack schedule for a minute, but then I've got a couple errands to run. We'll be back at 5:30 to pick you up. Have fun out there."

"Sounds good, Mom. You know I will." Regan grabbed her drawstring bag, kissed Sam on the forehead, and ran out onto the field. This was the second year they'd practiced at Wolf Trails Park. It only had one field on a hill next to the playground. Regan could see Leslie and Conor helping their dad set up the cones for dribbling drills. The twins' dad had been their coach since preschool. Regan adored him. He was a goalie in college and still played on what he called the Geezer Squad.

The teams had been co-ed when they were younger, so Regan had played with Conor, too. Once he'd actually tried to help her score, but tackled her into the goal along with the ball instead.

She wasn't unhappy when he'd switched to playing lacrosse and basketball. He still liked to help his dad out, though, whenever he didn't have a practice of his own. Fortunately, Coach Pete usually shooed him off to run laps. That way the girls didn't have to listen to his "expert" advice all practice.

Regan set her bag down just as Conor yelled, "Think fast!" and kicked a ball in her direction. At the same time, Leslie cartwheeled over. She landed in front of Regan with a dramatic, "Ta-da!" Regan stuck a foot out in a half-hearted attempt to get the ball but she was more interested in getting Leslie's attention.

Her friend just never stood still for long. Leslie ignored her until Coach Pete caught his daughter by the leg and hung her upside down for a minute. He set her down gently saying, "We're at soccer practice, darlin', not gymnastics." He squeezed Regan's shoulder.

"Welcome back, soccer star."

"Some star," said Conor. "She let that ball go right by her when she could have easily passed it back to me."

Regan started to object, but Coach Pete cut them both off.

"That's enough, Conor. Please go get the bag of extra balls out of the trunk so we can get practice started."

As Conor hustled down the hill, Regan turned to Leslie who was now doing spinning jumping jacks.

"How do you put up with him?" Regan asked as Leslie dropped dizzily to the ground. "Oh, never mind. What I really want to know is did you open your tool kit? I almost forgot about soccer practice I was so excited to get started on it." She kept her voice to a whisper, even though the coach was well out of earshot. He preferred the girls to have their heads in the game when they were on the field.

"Nope, my dad was already loading up the car when we got off the bus. I barely had a chance to change and grab my cleats before he and Conor were out of the driveway." She rolled her eyes. "You know how crazy my dad is at the start of a new season. So...what's in it?"

"No idea, but I'm dying to know what kind of tools we could possibly need for school. I mean we already bought most of our own supplies. What else is there?"

"Maybe there's a glue gun to keep Conor in his seat," Leslie said as her brother arrived with the bag of soccer balls. That made Regan laugh out loud.

"Now that would make third grade awesome

for sure!"

A silvery blue mini-van pulled up alongside the field. The automatic door slid back with a whir and a click as four pony-tailed girls tumbled out.

"Looks like the carpool has arrived with the rest of the team," said Coach Pete. "Bring it in, girls. Let's get this season underway."

There were only two new girls on the team this year. The other seven were on at least their second season together. They didn't need to spend much time getting to know each other or the drills. Still, everybody was a little rusty, and Regan was especially off her game. After her third missed pass, Coach Pete pulled her aside.

"Regan, where's your head today? Your feet are on the field, but your brain seems a little distracted."

"Sorry Coach. I guess I'm still thinking about school today. I'll do better." *It's that silly tool kit. I can't stop thinking about it.* But she pushed it out of her head and scored three goals in their final scrimmage.

At the end of practice, the girls were worn out, but it was a great kind of tired. They sat on the castle and bridge of the playground equipment to have their snacks. Coach Pete carried over a bright yellow, reusable tote bag from Joe's Pizza. He made a grand sweep with his arm, saying, "And now the moment you've all been waiting for. The unveiling of our uniform shirt." Regan held her breath. Each season, the town teams got a new uniform shirt. To keep it fair, the league organizers chose the colors randomly, so it was always a surprise.

Coach reached into the bag. In slow motion,

he pulled out the top shirt. "Voila!"

Navy. Ugh. Navy looks awful with black soccer shorts, Regan thought. She scanned the eight stony faces around her. No cheers for navy. *Darn. I was hoping for lime green shirts this year. I had a name picked out, too, the Lima Beans. Heh, Heh. I just crack myself up.*

Coach Pete ignored the lack of enthusiasm and got straight down to business. "Now we need to make a list of the numbers you each want and choose a team name. Hey, Regan, grab that clipboard over there and write down the numbers everyone wants on the roster. We'll choose in reverse alphabetical order by first name this year."

"Whoo-hoo," hollered Whitney Xavier, who almost never got to go first for anything. "I'd like to be lucky number sev-en!"

The girls all chose quickly and, surprisingly, without any squabbling over the numbers. "And I'll take 18 this year," said Regan handing the clipboard back to Coach.

"This year? More like every year," said Leslie laughing. "You're always 18."

Whitney, who was new to the team, asked, "What's so special about the number 18?"

"R is the 18th letter of the alphabet, of course. Regan likes to match," Leslie explained, using air quotes when she said the word "match."

"Oh, wow, that's kind of cool, Regan," said Whitney. "I like that idea so much. Could you change me to number 23?"

"Why yes, yes I can, Whitney," said Regan smiling smugly at Leslie and taking the clipboard back from Coach Pete.

"Okay…Okay," Coach Pete said. "Now,

who's got an idea for a team name?"

"Razzle Dazzle!"

"Wizards!"

"Thunder!"

"Purple Panthers!"

No, no, no, and OMG—no! Every year it was the same silliness. Regan fought to keep her frustration from showing when Caroline suggested the Hello Kitties. How dopey was that?

"How about the Pokemon Pirates?" Maddie asked.

Regan wasn't the only girl who groaned at that one. *Why was Maddie so obsessed with her brother's card collection, anyway?* Regan wondered. *Help, Coach Pete! Please don't let us end up with something really embarrassing like the Pink Flamingos. Why are everyone's ideas always so lame? I wonder if they'd like my idea though. What if they don't get it or make fun of it? Ugh.*

Before she could work up the courage to share her idea, Conor interrupted. "Hey," he hollered from the grass just beyond the playground where he was bouncing a ball off his knees. "Shouldn't you try and pick a name that goes with your shirt color? You know, like last year you were the Flames because you had red shirts?"

Geesh, thought Regan, *you know you're in trouble when Conor's the only one making any sense.* Regan very softly offered the name she'd been mulling over. "What about the Navy SEALs?" She looked around for a reaction from the team.

Caroline looked a little confused. Maddie stretched out her arms, clapped the backs of her hands together, and started barking, "Arp, arp, arp." All the girls laughed.

"Not that kind of seal, you goofball. I'm talking about a military SEAL."

"They have seals in the military? Wha-a-tt?" Sarah made her eyes bug out for effect.

"You're ridiculous," said Regan. "Seriously though, my uncle's a Navy SEAL, and they are the toughest team around. He does all sorts of secret missions he can't tell us about, but I know they are dangerous. He can do one hundred, one-armed push-ups faster than anything."

Coach Pete was nodding in approval (and so, Regan noticed, was Conor). "Navy SEALs, I like it. Short and sweet, but tough as nails. I think that suits this team to a tee. Whaddya think girls? All those in favor say 'Aye'. Actually, all in

33

favor say, 'Aye, Aye', like a sailor."

The girls moaned and tried some sloppy salutes. Coach Pete announced, "Okay, my super SEALs, I think our fleet has arrived to carry you home."

Regan spied a shiny red SUV in the sea of minivans. She raced to the car to tell her mom that their new team name had been her idea. Plus, she couldn't wait to get home and finally find out what was in her tool kit!

Chapter Three

Regan dumped her soccer bag in the mudroom and kicked her cleats under the bench.

"Straight to the showers for you, Reggie-roo," her mom called from the garage. "Daddy will be home in about 15 minutes, and dinner will be on the table in twenty."

"But, Mom, I just need 10 minutes to look at my tool kit."

Regan's mom answered with a gentle shove

of her foot on Regan's backside as she came through the door with the groceries. "After dinner. Now scoot."

Dinner was homemade pizza and fruit salad. Her mom made individual sized crusts, and everybody got to put on their own toppings. Regan's dad always made what he liked to call "garbage dump pizza"—it had a little bit of everything on it. Sam insisted on making his own pizza and then always refused to eat it. Regan made four different slices with one ingredient each: olive, mushroom, tomato, and one plain cheese.

Tonight, though, she barely tasted it; all she could think about was her tool kit. As soon as she was done, she asked to be excused.

"Go, go, go," said her mom, "but please clear your plate first."

Regan jumped down from her chair, dumped her plate and cup somewhat clumsily into the dishwasher, and ran to the little office she shared with her parents. The tall, wide desk in the middle nearly filled the whole room. She opened the closet to get some paper and a pencil from her homework supply bin. The desk had a chair on both sides. Regan always sat facing the door so Sam couldn't sneak up on her.

Her mom had moved her backpack and tool kit to the office while Regan changed for soccer. The bright bag stood out against the white desk. She managed to get the knot out of the ribbon fairly easily this time and gently emptied it out. A battery rolled to the edge of the desk, but she caught it before it fell to the floor. Moving it back to the center, she noticed it had a smiley face sticker on it. *How odd.*

There was also a wide green rubber band and two folded pieces of paper. Regan opened the first one to reveal a map. *Wait, is a map a tool? Or a rubber band for that matter? Oh, it's a map of our town, and that red star is our school. Well, that's cool. But I don't need a map to find my school—I've been going there for years. What in the world am I supposed to do with these?*

These were certainly not like the tools her dad kept out in the garage. There was no hammer, screwdriver, or even a pair of pliers. She was especially disappointed there wasn't a level, which was her favorite. She liked to watch the bubble slide around inside and make it stay exactly in the center. What was Ms. Eaton thinking?

She opened the second folded paper, but the

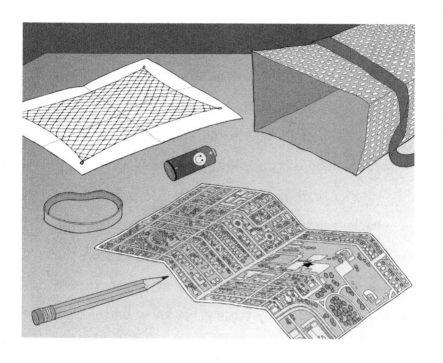

picture of a net didn't clear it up any. The directions asked her to explain how a battery, a rubber band, a map, and a net were going to help her be a first-rate third grader.

"I really have no clue," Regan said out loud. This year was going to be a challenge all right.

Regan's dad poked his head through the

door. "Mom tells me you've got some pretty interesting homework in third grade. Do you think I'm smart enough to understand it?"

"Dad, can I please tell you about it later? I really need to concentrate right now."

Her dad put on his sad face and started backing out the door. "Sor-ry, I'll just hang the Do Not Disturb—Genius at Work sign on the door as I leave." He winked at Regan so she knew he was only teasing. He knew better than anyone how seriously she took her schoolwork.

Regan stared blankly at her tools. She hadn't wanted to explain the tool kit to her dad because she really didn't understand it herself. She rubbed her eyes and wiggled in her chair. She thought about everything she'd done in second grade. They'd never had homework like this.

Oh shoot, what was it Mrs. Hoffman taught us

to do last year when we were stumped? I wish I'd asked Dad to stay. Oh wait, I know, brainstorm, that's it.

Brainstorming, Mrs. Hoffman had said, was like dumping out your brain. You were supposed to say or list every idea or connection you could make that might help you—no matter how silly or unrelated it seemed.

Fingering each of the tools like a piece of treasure, she finally settled on the battery. Regan sat up straight in her chair and squared her shoulders. "OK, what do I know about batteries?"

She wrote for a few minutes, and her list looked like this:

• use in alarm clocks, flashlights, radios, cameras and other stuff

• give power

• that bunny on the commercials that kept going & going…

• have a + and − sign on them (WHY does this one have a smiley face on it??)

• some are rechargeable

• batteries run out when you need them most − like in dad's phone

• mom says they're expensive and not to waste them

Regan tightened her pony tail and tapped her pencil on the desk. Finally she wrote:

Third graders need lots of energy for all the hard work they have to do.

She went through the same process for each of the other tools. About 20 minutes later, she thought she had answers that made sense. However, she wasn't at all sure they were the answers Ms. Eaton was looking for. That bothered her all night long. Regan not only liked to be ready, she liked to be right.

Chapter Four

The next morning, Leslie wasn't on the bus. According to Conor, she'd overslept and was going to make everybody but him late.

Aghh, I really wanted to talk to Leslie about that crazy tool kit before school. She couldn't believe her ears when she heard Conor tell Joaquin he'd had the easiest homework ever. "Third grade is going to be a piece of cake."

What??!

Ms. Eaton greeted Regan at the door. "Did you bring your tools to school today, Regan?" she asked with a grin.

Regan shrugged and whispered, "I have them Ms. Eaton. But I'm not sure I know exactly how to use them."

Ms. Eaton winked. "Not to worry, by the end of the morning you'll be a pro."

Regan hurried to her desk thinking, *I hope you're right, Ms. Eaton. I hope you're right.*

After the morning announcements, Ms. Eaton asked the children to get out their tool kits and their answer sheets. Projected on the big screen was a picture of the battery. "Let's start with this tool. Who noticed anything unusual about this particular battery?"

Aidan's hand shot up and he was talking before Ms. Eaton could call on him. "There's a smiley face near the plus sign."

"Why do you think that is, Aidan?" she asked.

Aidan raised both hands and shrugged.

¯_(ツ)_/¯

"I'll bet Gabi knows." Gabi scowled at Aidan. "Well, I know the plus sign means positive. And…if you're positive it can mean you're absolutely sure. I told my mom this morning that I was positive my sister drank some of my smoothie." She scrunched up her nose. "It was contaminated, for sure!"

"You're on the right track focusing on the positive," said Ms. Eaton. "Can anyone add to the great start Gabi gave us?"

Regan was still thinking about her answer when Aidan's hand rocketed into the air. Ms. Eaton called on him again.

"My football coach always tells us to have a positive attitude," he explained. "You know, like if you think you can score a touchdown and win the game, then you probably can. Like that little engine that kept saying, 'I think I can, I think I can,' until it got over the mountain."

"That's a great way to explain it, Aidan. A negative attitude gets in the way of a lot of good learning. I hope this year you will all be as excited about *learning* as you are about *knowing*."

Regan slouched in her seat. Her answer had been wrong. Her eyes filled with tears, and she pretended to sneeze so she could grab a tissue. Then she heard Ms. Eaton say, "That's one way the battery can help you have a great year, but I bet you all came up with some other great reasons. That's okay, too! Sometimes a question has lots of answers that work. Does anyone else want to share an idea about the battery?"

Ms. Eaton scanned the classroom. When she glanced at the Blue Dolphins table, Regan fidgeted with her pencil and didn't make eye contact. *Is energy a good answer? It has nothing to do with a positive attitude. Oh gosh, just give it a try already.*

But Ms. Eaton had already moved on to the next tool. A quick tap on her laptop and up popped a picture of a rubber band. "What about the rubber band? Why is that in your tool kit?" asked Ms. Eaton.

Leslie raised her hand about half way.

"Leslie, how do you think we can use that rubber band?"

"Well," said Leslie slowly, "rubber bands stretch, and they can hold things together...so maybe it's to keep us organized?"

"That's a terrific thought, Leslie. It sure helps to be organized." The children laughed as Ms. Eaton gestured at her own messy desk already piled with books and folders. "Did anyone come up with another idea?"

Regan read and reread her answer about the rubber band. She glanced over at Conor who was waving his hand wildly at the next table group. Even that couldn't convince her to volunteer an answer.

"Conor, I can't quite tell," Ms. Eaton said with a small smile, "do you have something you'd like to share?"

"Yes, finally!" shouted Conor. "I think the rubber band means we'll have to stretch our minds to hold lots of new information."

"Excellent answer. The third grade curriculum

is full of things you haven't learned before. You'll need some extra room to hold all these new facts and ideas. Good job, both of you."

Conor pumped his fist triumphantly, and Regan put her head in her hands. *That was almost exactly what I had written down. Why didn't I say anything?*

"Let's build on Conor's idea for a minute," Ms. Eaton continued. "Everyone please pick up your rubber band and stretch it out in front of you."

The class eagerly followed her direction. Conor pulled his rubber band so far it snapped and whizzed past Regan's nose. She glared at him, but he was too busy high fiving Max to notice.

"Okay class, hold your rubber bands steady. Now look around. Do you see what happened?"

She paused while the children craned their necks and lifted out of their seats to look at their classmates' rubber bands. "Max, what do you notice?"

"Well, Sarah is stretching it between her thumb and pinkie on one hand. And…well, Gabi and Owen used both hands but they are pulling in different directions. Hey—everybody did something different so…who did it right?"

"There is no one right way, and that's exactly the point. Everyone followed the directions, but in different ways. I hope our class will be full of *flexible* thinkers. You know sometimes we love our own idea so much we don't really listen to, or appreciate, other ideas. We're going to work on that this year, too." Ms. Eaton glanced at the wall clock. "Yikes, we're running behind, and it's almost time for gym. Please put your tool kits in

51

your desk. We'll have to finish the last two tools tomorrow morning."

The classroom erupted in a chorus of disappointed grumblings.

"How about after lunch, Ms. Eaton? Couldn't we talk about them then?" begged Conor.

"Sorry, Conor. Our afternoon will be full of math and science. You'll all have to wait for tomorrow."

Regan tucked her tools into her desk. She was relieved she'd get to think about the map and the net again tonight when she worked on the rest of her homework. She thought she'd ask her dad to brainstorm with her this time.

But even her favorite subjects couldn't keep her mind off her tool kit. All afternoon she kept thinking about maps and nets instead of multiplication and simple machines. She barely said a word to Leslie on the bus ride home. She refused to play Hungry Hungry Hippos with Sam, even though it was secretly still one of her favorite games. To make matters worse, her dad had to work a little later than usual. By the time dinner was over, he didn't have much time to brainstorm with Regan before she had to get ready for bed.

He looked at the tools and listened carefully as Regan explained what went on in class that morning. He smiled as he read over her answers.

"Reggie-roo, I think you're exactly on track. These are terrific ideas. Maybe I should get a tool kit for the office, so I wouldn't have to work late so often. What do you think?" He tickled her under the ribs and made her squirm.

"I think you're not much help tonight, Dad."

She pushed her papers away from her and laid her head on the desk.

"Regan, we've talked about this before. You don't have to do everything perfectly. All you can do is try your best and learn from your mistakes. We all make them, you know."

"But Dad, I don't *like* making mistakes," Regan said, frowning at him.

"I think it's time for you to sleep on it. You can look over your answers again tomorrow morning while you're having your pancakes."

Regan's head popped up at the mention of her favorite breakfast. "Pancakes! Are you staying for breakfast tomorrow, Dad?"

"You bet, and no box mix for me. We can make them together from scratch. Now get upstairs; Mom and I will be up in a minute to tuck you in."

"What about blueberries?" asked Regan.

"What *about* blueberries?" answered her dad.

"Daa-aad," Regan moaned, "do we have blueberries for the pancakes? You know they're my favorite."

"Oh, you like blueberries in your pancakes, do you? Well then, we shall all have blueberries in our pancakes tomorrow."

Giving him a kiss and hug, Regan flew up the steps, forgetting her frustration with her tool kit. She was too busy picturing a big plate of blueberry pancakes (with no syrup, thank you very much). She'd have to ask her mom if they could have bacon, too.

Chapter Five

The next morning, her dad was already busy in the kitchen when Regan got downstairs. Sam had his apron on and was standing on a chair helping stir the batter.

"Good morning, Sunshine. Meet Sammy, my sous chef," said her dad, who was making a mess sure to earn him some teasing. Regan giggled as Sam made a deep bow with his spoon and managed to get pancake batter in his hair.

"Hey, can you grab the baking powder out of the pantry so I can get these pancakes on the griddle?"

Regan looked on the shelf where her mom kept the flour, sugar, and other baking supplies. There was no baking powder.

"Dad, we have baking soda, but I think we're out of baking powder." Regan slumped against the pantry door feeling like she might cry. "Oh no, does this mean no pancakes?"

"Hey buck up, kiddo. That is not a problem for this guy. Bring me that baking soda, and see if we have any cream of tartar in the spice drawer."

Regan pulled open the drawer of conveniently alphabetized spices. She found the cream of tartar between the cinnamon and cumin, and handed it to her dad.

"We can substitute these two ingredients in place of the baking powder," he explained. "Pretty slick, huh?"

"How do you know that, Dad?"

"I learned it Down Under. You know, when I trekked across the Outback making pancakes for roving herds of kangaroos," he said using an awful Australian accent.

"Oh, really?" Regan played along. She was used to her dad's outrageous stories.

"Or, it's possible I Googled it the last time we were out of baking powder," he said with a wink.

"So when are these hoppin' good kangaroo pancakes going to be ready?" Regan asked, moving the blueberries out of Sam's reach so there'd be some left for the pancakes.

"Give me five minutes. Why don't you go

look over your tool kit answers while you're waiting for your plate of perfect pancakes?"

"No, I think you were right last night. Since Ms. Eaton thinks lots of answers work, I'm going to stick with the ones I have. I'll set the table so we'll be ready when Mom gets downstairs."

A few minutes later, breakfast was ready. Mr. Hines set a platter of perfectly round pancakes and crispy bacon in the center of the table. Then he placed a special pancake shaped like an "R" in front of Regan.

"Something smells awfully good," said Regan's mom as she entered the kitchen. Catching sight of the messy counters, she added, "And looks pretty awful. Whoa, that includes you, Sam!"

"No worries, honey, I'll clean up both Sam and the kitchen after we eat."

"I'll hold you to it." She pulled Regan's hair over her shoulder to keep it out of the syrup. "Regan, Dad's taking Sam to preschool today. I'm going right by your school on my way downtown so you don't have to gobble down your pancakes to make the bus. You've got at least ten extra minutes."

"That's great, Mom." Regan finished off the last bite of her pancake. "I'll have enough time for seconds." She served herself another and, as she spread butter all over it, she smirked. "Dad was about to tell me if kangaroos use syrup on their pancakes or not."

"Aren't you a silly Sheila this morning?" said her dad.

Her mom rolled her eyes at the accent and turned to help Sam cut up his pancakes.

"Seriously, though, Dad, these may be the

best pancakes you've ever made. Maybe we should skip the baking powder every time."

Regan's dad did a little victory dance around the kitchen island. Sam clapped his sticky hands together. They were stopped in their tracks by an unexpected shriek from her mom, who said, "Oh my, look at the clock! My watch must be slow."

Regan shoved her chair back in a panic. "Yikes, I'm going to be late if we don't leave right this minute! Dad, you'll have to clear my plate too. Sorry, thanks for a great breakfast."

And just like that, she dashed for the garage. Mrs. Hines scrambled to collect her purse and keys. With a quick kiss for Mr. Hines and Sam, she was out the door just as the car door slammed with Regan ready to go inside.

Chapter Six

Regan was excited to see the map of their town on the front screen when she breezed into the classroom. Thank goodness they'd get started on their tool kits right away. She had her tool kit and notes out and was ready to go before the late bell rang.

"Good morning, everyone."

"Good morning, Ms. Eaton!"

"We've got a full schedule today, so please

get the maps from your tool kits out. I have slightly different directions for each table group so listen carefully."

First she asked the Minecraft Mania table to find the fastest way to get from the school to the movie theater downtown. Then she instructed the Avengers to stop at the bank to get money to buy tickets. "How many blocks does that add to the trip?"

Regan already had her finger on the school on her map when Ms. Eaton turned to her table.

"Blue Dolphins, you need to pick up your friend on Elm Street first. What route would you take?"

Next, she asked the Flying Monkeys to take the scenic route along the river. "How does that change your route?" She finished her instructions by giving the Magic Jumping Beans and the Raptors the same directions. "Your drivers are nervous about the traffic on Main Street. Can you get there on side streets?"

The class got to work. At the Blue Dolphin table, Trevor was trying to find his house on the map, and Sarah was coloring the river blue. Not much was getting done. Regan was quietly drawing the map in her head and waiting impatiently for everyone else. Hearing Conor's voice over at the Avengers' table snapped her to attention. He was saying something about Beulah Road having too many stoplights. *Oh no, they are almost done!* Regan wasn't going to let him have all the glory this time. When Kenny started drawing teeny-tiny cars on the roads, she couldn't take it anymore.

"Trevor, put your finger on the school. Sarah,

put a finger on the movie theater. Elm Street is right here."

Her group jumped into action following Regan's direction. With everyone working together, they quickly figured it out.

After a few minutes, Ms. Eaton asked each group for one volunteer to draw their path on the large map. Regan shot her hand into the air, eager to be picked for this prime assignment, but she wasn't the only one. Ms. Eaton had lots of hands to choose from.

Ms. Eaton surveyed the classroom and called out, "Maria, Natalie, Ethan, Demetrius, Eunice and...Kenny. Please pick a different color marker to draw your team's route on the big map."

Regan slowly lowered her hand. Obviously, Ms. Eaton hadn't seen that Kenny's only contribution to their map had been silly little car drawings. And look, he'd picked up the red marker. Didn't he even know they were the *Blue* Dolphins? Ugh. Maybe third grade wasn't going to be so great after all.

"Okay, fabulous work as navigators everyone," said Ms. Eaton as Eunice finished the last of the routes. "You all got to the movie theater six different ways. But what did that exercise teach us? Why is the map in our tool kit?"

Regan sat up straight and pasted a hopeful look on her face, but Ms. Eaton's eyes slid past her.

"What do you think, Owen?" Owen looked nervously at his best friend Ethan who gave him the thumbs up sign. Owen took a deep breath. "We all started at the same place, AND we all ended at the same place. But we all went different ways to get there. That makes me think about math problems. There are lots of different ways to get the same answer. Like one plus five equals six—but so does two times three."

Ms. Eaton leaped off the edge of her desk where she'd been perched. "That's a terrific explanation, Owen. I couldn't have said it any better myself."

Owen blushed and slid down in his chair.

"But gosh, why would it ever be important to know all these different ways? Wouldn't one way be enough to get you there? Jalen, what do you think?" Ms. Eaton asked.

Jalen talked about the need to avoid traffic jams and accidents. This made Regan remember the pancakes her dad cooked that morning. He'd made a last minute substitution so they didn't have to eat cereal for breakfast. *Hey, he'd used the map tool without even realizing it.*

Ms. Eaton was now saying, "That's super Jalen; and you should always be looking for options in the classroom too. What else is a map good for?"

This time it was Owen nodding encouragingly at Ethan whose hand was halfway up.

"Yes, Ethan."

"If Owen figures out how to get to the movies, then he can tell me so we can go together. He can't eat all that popcorn by himself, you know."

"And how does that relate to our learning, Ethan?" coaxed Ms. Eaton.

"It's like when teachers say you have to show your work so they know how you got the answer. Otherwise you could just be a good guesser, I guess."

"Bingo! This year we're going to work on finding lots of ways to solve tough problems. And we'll practice explaining our thinking so everyone can understand. Now, I don't know about you, but my brain needs a break. We're going to have to finish up with our tool kits this afternoon." Ms. Eaton scratched her head. "We only have about 10 minutes before it's time for our first all school assembly. Let's all relax and read, anywhere you're comfortable, until we need to line up."

Ms. Eaton's class went straight from the assembly to lunch. Leslie and Regan had volunteered to go back to the classroom for the lunch bucket, but Ms. Eaton sent Max and Demetrius instead. Lunch had been a disaster.

First, Regan's mom had forgotten to write anything on her napkin. She always wrote a little note or drew a silly picture. Last year she'd even started giving Regan little puzzles to figure out. Regan looked forward to seeing what her mom came up with each day. She couldn't believe she'd already forgotten on the third day of school.

Just as Leslie was telling her how Hope had gotten in SO MUCH trouble for using her mom's makeup, the lunch ladies turned out all the lights in the cafeteria. This was the signal that everyone had to stop talking because some people had been too loud.

Of course, the main culprits were Conor and Kenny who were loud *and* messy. The poor janitor had to come with his mop to clean up the chocolate milk pond that had appeared under their table. The two of them had the nerve to act like they had no idea how that mess could have happened. Regan could read their lips from the next table. *It was an accident. Must have been spontaneous combustion. Gosh, we're so sorry.* Then they'd turned and made faces at their friends behind Mr. Jessop's back. So rude! They didn't even get in trouble. The lunch ladies totally believed the milk story. Regan knew better. Boys and straws were a bad combination.

The rest of the afternoon didn't go quite as planned either. Instead of finishing up their tool kits, they'd had their first fire drill. The deafening alarm went off just as they were finishing up their math lesson. It was a beautiful sunny day and no one minded standing outside, but every year the first drill took forever. One new teacher always left without her class list. One fifth grader always stayed in the bathroom. To make matters worse, they'd had to repeat the drill two extra times. Why? Because Conor and Kenny could not be still *and* quiet for even five minutes.

Chapter Seven

Ms. Eaton started the day Friday saying, "I have a surprise for all of you. At our teacher's meeting yesterday, Mr. Morris and I decided we couldn't wait until next week to introduce you to your reading buddies. We're going to do it this morning. Isn't that great? They'll be arriving with their books in a few minutes."

Mr. Morris had been Regan's first grade teacher but now he taught kindergarten. Third grade was the first year you got to be a book buddy instead of have a book buddy. The pairings were always kindergarten and third grade, first and fourth, and second and fifth. It was a big responsibility. Regan had learned a lot from her wonderful book buddies over the years. She couldn't wait to read all her old favorite stories to her new little buddy.

"When they get here," Ms. Eaton was saying, "we'll have them sit on the reading rug, and then Mr. Morris will read off the pairings. The kindergarten class is a little smaller than ours. Some of these lucky kiddos will actually get two book buddies!"

On cue, the door opened. They could hear Mr. Morris's booming voice before they saw him.

"Are you read-y for some read-ing?"

"Yes we are! Yes we are!" the whole class

chanted. The kindergartners filed in looking a little frightened by all the noise the big kids were making.

"Okay, okay, let's settle down, boys and girls. My kiddos need to park it on that rug and get all crisscross applesauce. Marcus, my man what's shakin'?" asked Mr. Morris, hip checking the chair of one of his past students.

He gave Regan a wiggly-fingered wave as he said, "Okay, let's get this party started!"

Reading from his clipboard, Mr. Morris jumped right in. "Clev-or Trev-or, you are going to work with my main man Roscoe over here. Roscoe's real name is Regis but I like to call him Roscoe." Regis/Roscoe playfully punched Mr. Morris as he walked over to Trevor's table, but Regan could tell he liked the attention.

"Leslie, girlfriend, let me introduce you to

Miss Maggie from Maple Rd. Maggie eats red Skittles for breakfast to keep her hair that fiery color and likes to wear her socks inside out." Maggie blushed and dropped her head into her lap, but she was smiling. Leslie walked over to the rug, sat down behind her, and tapped her on the shoulder. Maggie was in her lap so fast she almost knocked her over.

Mr. Morris had something silly to say about every child in his class and a few of the third graders, too. The kids all loved him. Regan counted the students who hadn't yet been matched up. There were three kindergartners on the rug and five third graders in their seats. She was just thinking how much fun it would be if she and Maria could work with Natalie's curly-haired little sister when she heard Mr. Morris say the unthinkable.

"Regan and Conor, today is your lucky day! Come meet Rob-Rob-Robyn before she starts bob-bob-bobbin' along."

Regan couldn't believe her ears. Mr. Morris should know better than anyone that she and Conor couldn't work together. Didn't he remember he'd had to move their desks to opposite sides of the room because Conor made her cry almost every day? Didn't he remember Conor loved to jump up and yell, "Done. Beat'cha again, Regan!" every time they did their Math Minute drills? Didn't he remember Conor tore up one of her tests when she got the highest score in the class? Regan certainly remembered, and the last thing she wanted was to work with Conor—even if Robyn was already on her feet and looking awfully excited about it all.

And there was Mr. Morris waiting for her. She certainly couldn't disappoint him by making a scene. Maybe she could talk to him later about making a switch, but for now she'd have to be a good sport. Just behind Mr. Morris's head she saw the battery picture Ms. Eaton had stuck on the bulletin board. *Have a positive attitude*, she reminded herself, taking a deep breath. She was putting her hand out to shake Robyn's already outstretched hand, when Conor ducked in front of her and grabbed both of Robyn's hands.

"Rockin' Robyn, it is a pleasure to meet you. My name's Conor. We are going to have a great time together." Finding an open spot on the rug, he and Robyn sat down. Conor pointed his thumb at Regan. "Oh and this is Regan, she'll pick out good books because she loves, loves, loves to read."

Robyn beamed at both of them and pushed her book into Conor's hands.

"Oh, *The Runaway Bunny*, that's a classic all right."

Regan sat on the other side of Robyn, feeling very much like the third wheel on a bicycle. She had looked forward to being a book buddy for so long, but this definitely wasn't what she had in mind.

Robyn grabbed her hand. "Look Regan, Conor drew me a bunny." And sure enough, there was a perfect drawing of a sweet bunny that Conor had sketched out on piece of scrap paper.

"That's Robyn Rabbit. Maybe we can all write a story about her next time," said Conor.

Robyn looked at him adoringly. "Oh, I'd like that. Will you help us Regan? Maybe there could

be another rabbit named Regan if that's okay with Conor?"

"That sounds like a super idea," said Regan, purposefully not making eye contact with Conor. She tried hard not to sound mean. Wasn't he just full of great ideas? She was going to need a bigger battery to get through Book Buddies every week.

The rest of the half hour went smoothly enough with Conor and Regan taking turns reading aloud to Robyn. They had just turned the last page when Mr. Morris clapped his hands. In his jolly voice he said, "Kinderkids, say thank you to your buddies, and let's make a bee-line for the dee-door!"

Robyn gave her buddies a hug—Conor first, Regan was quick to note. All the kindergartners lined up like they'd been doing it their whole lives instead of just four days. Mr. Morris was a miracle worker. Everyone said so.

Chapter Eight

They hadn't been gone two minutes when Ms. Eaton found Mr. Morris's clipboard on the top of the bookshelf. "Oops, he's going to need this. Regan and Conor, please take a hall pass and return this to him. He's in Room 12 down by the art room this year. I think he had something he wanted to share with you two, anyway."

Conor lunged for the clipboard, leaving Regan to grab the hall pass off its hook by the door. Ms. Eaton didn't use the school issued passes. She hand-painted her own and they were little miniature works of art. She felt it made the students take better care of them. She hadn't lost even one in eight years of teaching.

"Don't run in the hallway, but hurry back, we've GOT to finish up our tool kits this morning."

Regan and Conor didn't say one word to each other and yet, somehow, managed to get in an argument on the short trip to Mr. Morris's room. Regan wanted to go down the stairs near their classroom, and Conor wanted to use the far staircase. Standing perfectly still with her arms folded, Regan finally convinced Conor to follow her. They had to stay together, after all. They risked losing their hall pass privileges if anyone saw them walking the halls alone.

Seeing them at the door with his clipboard, Mr. Morris laughed and said, "Oh my goodness, I'd lose my head if it wasn't stapled on!"

Conor and Regan giggled. They both missed Mr. Morris. He somehow managed to make everything seem fun. His class was in the middle of free play.

"I really miss free play," said Conor.

"I'm sure Ms. Eaton's got important third grade stuff waiting for you, Con-man. Actually, though, I'm glad you're both here. I wanted to share a little info about your reading buddy."

He pulled them a little further away from the play area and dropped his voice to a whisper. "Robyn has a learning disability called dyslexia, which makes it super hard for her to learn to read. That's why I gave her two of my smartest students to work with this year. I know she's going to do great with you two on her side. I may have you take turns coming to the classroom to help her with specific assignments if you're cool with that."

"Can you assign her to build something with Legos when I come?" asked Conor.

Regan rolled her eyes. "Of course, we'd love to do anything we can, Mr. Morris." She elbowed Conor who chimed in with an enthusiastic, "Well sure, whatever you need, Mr. M." He rubbed his side and moved a little further away from Regan.

"I knew I could count on my two reading rock stars. Here's a little bit of information for you to read up on dyslexia, but we can talk more about it next week." He handed Regan a pamphlet, and then led them to the door. "You guys better get back to class before Ms. Eaton accuses me of trying to steal her students. She knows I'd take you back in a heartbeat."

On the way back to Room 23, Regan and Conor couldn't stop talking about dyslexia.

"Whoa, I'm glad dyslexia wasn't part of the spelling bee last year," said Conor. "You don't see too many words with a y and an x like that."

"No kidding," agreed Regan.

"I can't even remember learning how to read," said Conor. "It just seems like I always knew how."

"Same here," said Regan. "I can't imagine how frustrating it would be to not be able to read by yourself. I like having my parents read me stories, but it's more fun to read alone. Let's ask Ms. Eaton if we can have some computer time to research dyslexia." She said the word slowly, working hard to pronounce it right.

"That's a great idea. We have to make sure we do all we can to help Robyn, right Regan?"

For the first time Regan could remember, she and Conor agreed on something other than how much they both liked Leslie and sports. She felt her lips tug into a grin.

Ms. Eaton was waiting at the door watching for them. "Thanks for running that errand, you two. Now if everyone will please lock your eyes on the screen." It was still lit up with the picture of the map from their tool kit. "And last but not least…"

The map faded, and a picture of a net twirled into its place. Under the net were the words, *Leap, and the net will appear.*

"I'll admit this is a tough one. Anybody want to give it a try?"

Regan flattened her answer sheet out with

her hand. She no longer thought what she'd written was so great. A new idea popped into her head, and she worked to get her thoughts together. Finally, she raised her hand.

"Regan, good for you. How're we going to use our nets this year?" asked Ms. Eaton.

Regan's voice caught a little as she said, "I think the leap part means we have to give new and even hard things a try. The net will catch us if we make a mistake. So I guess that means it's okay to be wrong sometimes?" Regan looked at her lap. She was a little afraid of what Ms. Eaton might say next.

Ms. Eaton clapped her hands and said, "Give that girl a gold star! Of course you can be wrong sometimes."

Regan's head popped up, and she beamed at Ms. Eaton, who leaned toward the class and looked slyly from side to side. "I'll let you in on a little secret...even I'm wrong sometimes. And, it's okay!" She laughed. "It's more than okay—it's expected. Sometimes one person's wrong answer leads the rest of us to the best answer. So you can't be afraid to say the wrong thing. This classroom is a safe place. You can take a risk here, because we're a team... a problem-solving team."

Regan sat up straight in her chair and nodded slightly to acknowledge her smiling tablemates.

Ms. Eaton looked up from her laptop as she finished closing the file. "By the way, exactly who is it that uses this kind of net to keep them safe as they perform?" she asked.

Out of the corner of her eye Regan saw Conor's hand shoot up, just as she heard Ms.

Eaton say, "Regan?" She couldn't help but glance smugly at Conor. Seeing the disappointed look on his face, though, made her feel a little more generous. "I think Conor's hand was up before mine, Ms. Eaton."

"Well, okay then, Conor," said Ms. Eaton giving Regan a quizzical look. "What do you know about safety nets?"

"Circus performers use them. They're called trapeze artists or high wire walkers. My mom and I read a book about a family called the Flying Wallendas who traveled all over the world doing daredevil stunts."

"Exactly. But wait, trapeze artists are experts. Why do they need a net, Regan?"

Regan was surprised to be called on, but knew a thing or two about circus acts, too.

"They weren't always experts. It takes a lot

of practice to do all those amazing tricks. It's very risky and sometimes they make mistakes. Actually, the Flying Wallendas didn't use their net when they performed. It's one of the reasons their act was so dangerous, and they became famous."

"Well, it's a good thing we'll have our nets while we are becoming third grade experts this year," said Ms. Eaton. "They'll allow us to take risks and make mistakes as we learn to do amazing things."

Ms. Eaton took a deep breath. "Thank you for all your great thinking this morning. It's almost time for music, but before we line up, let me say thank you for a great first week of school. I'm really excited by all you've already learned and by the curiosity you've shown. I think we are going to have a terrific year in third grade."

"Of course we're going to have a great year," said Owen. "We've got you and our tool kits to help us."

Ethan chimed in with, "Yeah, what he said!"

The whole class laughed and gave Ms. Eaton a big thumbs up. Ms. Eaton added a picture of the net to the now full bulletin board she'd titled: Always Bring Your Tools to School.

Regan carefully put all her tools back into their colorful bag. She knew she had already used the net today. It took a little bit of courage to answer that last question even though she wasn't sure she was right.

She and Conor were definitely going to need their maps if they were going to find lots of different ways to help their new friend Robyn learn to read. She'd even sort of used the rubber band when her friends had been suggesting silly names for their soccer team.

It had been a great first week in third grade. Regan couldn't wait until next week to find other ways she could use her tools. She gently tucked the bag inside her desk and hurried to join her friends in line.

"Are we ready?" asked Ms. Eaton, meaning ready for music.

"You bet," answered Regan with a big smile. She was starting to believe she was ready for anything!

How to Make Your Own Tool Kit

Hey, you finished the book! That's so great. What now? Well, you could just read it again. Or you could make your own tool kit. It's really not too hard. You can always use the picture on page 39 to help you draw your own version of each tool. Or, if you've got access to a computer and printer, follow the directions below.

1) **Find a battery.** It's better to use a dead one, since that's like recycling. Please don't take one that's working out of the TV remote, for instance. Can't find one? No problem. If you Google "cartoon battery" you'll find lots of fun options. You can either print your favorite or use it as inspiration to draw your own. Don't forget the smiley face!

2) **Find a rubber band.** Try the junk drawer—every house has one. Any size will work. Even the one from your brother's braces will work in a pinch (maybe before he uses it though). They also come on asparagus in the produce section of the grocery store, and it's never a bad idea to eat more vegetables.

3) **Print a map.** Any map will do as a reminder to try lots of different ways to get to the same place. Google "neighborhood maps for kids" for fun versions—even some you can color yourself.

4) **The net** is probably the trickiest tool. You can Google "circus net" to find some good pictures of the nets that encourage us to take safe risks.

5) **Find a paper bag** and some ribbon or string and fill it up with your tools. If the bag isn't fancy, well, decorate it! With crayons, markers, or stickers and a dash of imagination of course.

Send a picture of you and your toolkit to me at rhymeswithchevy@gmail.com, and every month I'll post reader pictures on my website (alisonlevey.com).

Thanks so much for reading *Ready, Regan?* I loved writing it and hope you loved reading it,

Alison

Alison Levey started her academic career as an elementary school teacher, but now she lives and works in the shadow of the golden dome at the University of Notre Dame in Indiana.

Given the long, cold winters in her part of the world, she likes to read on her front porch, dine "al fresco," and ride her bike whenever she can. As a writer, Alison especially likes to play with silly rhymes, alliteration, and acronyms. Her two greatest loves and inspirations are her husband, Brian, and their son, Conor.

You can find out more about Alison's background, writing, and current work with college students on www.alisonlevey.com.

Karyn Lewis is an illustrator, writer, crafter, mom, and wife. She received a Bachelor of Fine Arts degree in drawing from Colorado State University, and worked in the newspaper industry for a number of years before focusing her attention on her freelance career. She currently lives in South Bend, Indiana, with her husband, Jeremy, and their son, William. To see more of her work visit www.karynlewis.com.